CULDESAC

Mike Nagel

autofocus books
Orlando, Florida

Published by Autofocus Books
autofocuslit.com

1st printing

Essay/Literature
ISBN: 978-1-957392-27-1

Library of Congress Control Number: 2023948116

CULDESAC

For J again.

And a little bit for O and M.

“The treadmill is a corollary to the suburb… a device with which to go nowhere in places where there is nowhere to go.”

—Rebecca Solnit, *Wanderlust: A History of Walking*

I heard an ad for a mattress company on a podcast the other day that said we spend one third of our lives sleeping but conveniently ignored what seems to me *the real issue here*, which is what to do about the two thirds of our lives we spend awake, just sort of walking around.

I spend ten years drinking Bulliet bourbon and eating Totino's Pizza Rolls. On Friday I get the results of my mandatory, in-office health screening. I score a 6.5 out of 10. My official health status in the eyes of my company is: ROOM FOR IMPROVEMENT. I'm at risk of all the usual killers—heart disease; hypertension; functional alcoholism; raging, merciless depression; obscure forms of diabetes — most of which I already have.

"How would you rate your stress level?" the nurse asked me.
"Non-existent," I said. "Everything in my life is a huge joke."

To keep us all alive and productive for as long as possible, my company offers us a free subscription to a fitness app called LIMEADE. A one-dollar value. Three times a day I'm prompted to participate in various activities designed to improve my overall health and wellbeing.

"Think a positive thought," it offers for 25 points. "Eat a banana," it offers for 30 points.

If I reach 2500 points, I unlock CRUNCH MODE and my company will cover 25% of my healthcare costs. A not-insignificant expense considering the rising cost of healthcare and the declining state of my health.

"It's not about how high your cholesterol is," my co-worker Amy tells me at lunch. "It's about how much cholesterol your body can *handle*."

"It is?" I say.

I never know what things are about. Every time someone tells me what something is about I'm always shocked.

That? I think. *That's* what it's about?

We're eating at Ascension, this soup and sandwich place near my office. It's in one of these new live/work/shop areas that are so trendy right now. Everything you need within walking distance. Your entire life in a two-block radius. While they were building this place, I used to come down here on my lunch break to walk in circles around the pond. I'd watch men and women in hard hats and reflective vests rearrange the surface of the Earth with Bobcats and back hoes. Sometimes I'd pretend I was telling them what to do.

"Put more dirt over there!" I'd yell.

"What!" they'd yell.

"Nothing!" I'd yell.

No matter how out of control your life feels it's always possible to act like you're still running the show. I once saw a toddler at a firework show pointing up at the sky like he was conducting the New York Philharmonic. According to developmental psychologists, it takes a newborn human nine months to realize that its actions can affect the world. Then another thirty-four years for it to realize that no, actually, they can't.

At Ascension, Amy and I both eat fancy grilled cheese sandwiches. What makes them fancy is how much cheese they put on them. Here's a fine dining tip for you. The more cheese they put on something the fancier it is.

"How do you find out how much cholesterol your body can handle?" I say.

"They have a test you can take," she says. "It's called the Denny's All-You-Can-Eat Grand Slam Breakfast Special. $7.99 on Saturdays. $6.99 if you're over sixty-five."

As a thirty-four-year-old poorly functioning diabetic with a history of high blood pressure and questionable-at-best eating habits, I should probably be more interested in things like cholesterol. For example, I should probably find out what it is. I know that, like most things, it comes in two kinds: good and bad. And I know that, like most things, it can kill you.

Sunday morning, I go to Whole Foods to stock up on the usual health essentials. Health food. Health booze. Health chocolate chip cookies. Health AAA batteries.

"Just because you buy it at Whole Foods doesn't mean it's healthy," my wife, J, says.

J's cute but I don't think she gets how Whole Foods works.

The lady at the checkout counter looks like healthy Kathy Bates. She's checked me out before. I remember because she looks like healthy Kathy Bates. And because she always checks my ID.

"1987," she always says. "Same as my son."

[]

It's early December. Our street is wall-to-wall inflatable snowmen. This is our first Christmas in this neighborhood. We didn't know what to expect. We should have expected more inflatable snowmen. At night they sway back and forth with these lunatic looks on their faces. In the morning, they're all deflated puddles of nylon, just their top hats sticking up out of the ground. It's a warm winter. Highs in the 80s. Lows in the 70s. We bundle up anyway. Hats and scarves and fingerless gloves.

"I dress for the weather I want," J says. "Not the weather I have."

At night I turn the air conditioner down to 70. The whole house rattles and hums. I sleep best when I'm warm in a cold place. I buy more blankets on Amazon.com. I buy a space heater. I spend a fortune keeping this place cold. Then I spend a fortune keeping us warm.

"Have you ever thought about working for yourself?" an entrepreneur once asked me when he found out I wrote advertising copy for a living.

"Why would I do that when I've spent so much time and energy learning how to work *against* myself?" I said.

For breakfast I make pre-cooked, microwavable bacon. You microwave it for five seconds.

For crispier bacon, the instructions say, *microwave for seven seconds.*

In an effort to not just up and die any day now, I've been cutting down on red meat, red wine, red sauce, Red Vines. Let me put it this way. If it's red, I'm cutting down on it.

I tell myself I'll just have two pieces of bacon. Then I microwave four pieces of bacon.

Well, I think, *it would be a waste not to eat all four pieces of bacon, seeing as they've already been microwaved.*

[]

On Christmas Day, we drive to J's parents' house. They live in West Plano, not far from us, in a neighborhood where all the houses are one story and everyone drives brand new Jeep Wranglers. Neither of us have made it very far from home. J's parents live fifteen minutes in one direction. My parents live fifteen minutes in the other direction. Me and J live right in the middle. I read on news.google.com that six in ten young adults live within ten minutes of their childhood home. Eight in ten live within thirty. It's perfectly normal, over the course of a lifetime, to not get anywhere.

On Christmas morning it's eighty-three degrees and sunny. My five-year-old niece asks me why it's hot in the winter.

"Oh, I don't know, Amanda," I say. "Maybe because the world is ending?"

I never know what to say to kids. I don't know what they want to hear. And I don't know how they want to hear it. J's getting her PhD in educational psychology. She says I should talk to them like adults.

"Yep," I say to Amanda. "Things sure aren't looking good future-wise."

[]

Lacking confidence in my ability to survive another year, I recently took out a million-dollar life insurance policy on myself. In the event that I just up and die, J will become a millionaire. They'll send her a check. Apparently a thirty-four-year-old buying a million-dollar life insurance policy on himself raises a few questions. I am sent, via email, a questionnaire:

- Do you plan on living the longest, healthiest life you possibly can?
- Do you generally enjoy being here and would prefer to drag this thing out as long as possible?
- Do you own a double-barreled shotgun, snub nose revolver, or have access to maybe a little too much prescription medication?

- Do you see where we're going with this?
- Are you going to make us say it?

When I get to the question about cholesterol, I explain to the questionnaire that it's not about how high my cholesterol is, it's about how much cholesterol my body can handle. My denial letter arrives five days later in an unmarked envelope from Nebraska.

"Looks like you're going to have to become a millionaire the old-fashioned way," I tell J, pouring myself another glass of whiskey, laying on our old, piece-of-crap couch.

"I thought cashing in on your dead husband's life insurance policy *was* the old-fashioned way," she says.

"Oh," I say. "Then I guess you're going to have to do it some new kind of way then."

[]

Sunday morning I wake up so hungover I have an out of body experience. That's convenient. My body is no place for me to be right now. It's been declared uninhabitable. I'm the one who declared it. I just kind of float around the room for a while, thinking about stuff.

"You live too much inside your own head," a cute girl in high school once told me.

"Why would I want to live anywhere else?" I said. "My head is accommodating! My head is tropical! It's 97 degrees in here all year round!"

I spend Sunday eating minestrone soup from

Whole Foods and having mild, hangover-induced panic attacks. The dog stands on my chest and licks my face. I wonder if he knows something I don't. Our dog isn't very smart but sometimes I think he can see the future. We got him nine years ago from a no-kill shelter in Downtown Plano, not far from where we live now. He's a Plano native. A schnauzer terrier mutt with grey fur and a head the size of an NBA basketball. The name on his paperwork was Argo but J changed it to Ollivander, after the wandmaker in Harry Potter. Ollie for short. A couple times a year he has seizures. He gets this crazy look on his face then stumbles around the house like an alcoholic. Sparklehead, we call it. Recently the vet told us it was time to change his food to some new, scientifically enhanced formula.

"Is it because of Sparklehead?" we said.

"No," he said. "It's because he's old."

[]

The spiritual writer Anne Lamott says there are only two kinds of prayers: "Help me, help me, help me," and "Thank you, thank you, thank you." I don't believe in prayer anymore, but I think she might be onto something. Gratitude and desperation. Back and forth.

In January the heat comes in waves. The cold comes in fronts. On Tuesday it's 75 degrees. On Thursday it's 29. I spend five days detoxing, then five days re-toxing.

"It's not about how much whiskey I drink," I yell to J from the couch. "It's about how much whiskey I can handle."

Back at my health screening, my doctor asked if I'd heard of Blue Zones.

"*Yes,*" I said.

Later I looked it up. It's these places in the world where people live to be a hundred years old. Low blood pressure. Low cholesterol. Low instances of people blowing their brains out with double barreled shotguns. The secret, Wikipedia said, is eating fish. They call the diet *The Holy Mackerel.*

On Wednesday I go to Whole Foods and announce that "I AM HERE FOR THE MACKEREL." I'm directed to the back counter where I talk to a middle-aged man named Tom. I tell Tom I need twenty-seven mackerels.

"Twenty-seven," I repeat slowly.

At the checkout counter, Healthy Kathy Bates rings up twenty-seven mackerels, three bags of gummy worms, two cases of Sierra Nevada Pale Ale, a six-pack of Tony's Chocolonely chocolate bars, an oversized cinnamon roll. Rather than abstain from bad things, I'm going to balance them out with good things instead. Drink a whiskey, eat a mackerel. Drive a gas-powered car, eat a mackerel. Net zero. Like I was never here. I show Healthy Kathy Bates my ID. "Same as your son," I say, and she looks pretty freaked out.

[]

I spend the weekend drinking bourbon and eating mackerel. The house smells like dead fish and cheap booze.

"This is a blue zone now," I announce, about the living room.

"This is a blue zone now too," I announce, about the bathroom.

"Blue zone, blue zone, blue zone," I go around announcing.

"Just because you're eating fish and making announcements doesn't mean you're in a blue zone," J says.

J's smart but I don't think she gets how announcements work. I don't think she gets how fish work either. She must have skipped those days in her super-fancy PhD program. Some things you can only learn from experience. Like how you can drink half a bottle of bourbon and four beers every night for seven years before you start to wonder if maybe you have a little problem on your hands. Or like how you can eat mackerel twelve days in a row before your pee starts to smell weird. Or like how you can say, "Help me, help me, help me," or "Thank you, thank you, thank you," but eventually those start sounding the same.

Recently J and I moved to East Plano, into a quiet neighborhood with a fantasy theme. One street is called Princess. One is called Camelot. We rented an old house on a cul-de-sac called Majestic Circle. Our house has three bedrooms, a breakfast nook, scratched-up hardwood floors, an overgrown backyard that's mostly mud. The backyard, we decided, is a project. One of many. When you're thirty-four and you don't have kids the thing you do have is projects. "I'm working on my projects," you tell yourself. "My projects require my attention."

One of the projects that requires my attention is this whole backyard situation. The other one is my life. Both seem to just be happening willy nilly.

"Willy nilly?" my counselor says.

"Willy *nilly*," I say.

I don't really have a counselor. I have a guy I bring my laptop to when it's acting funny. Terry in IT. Sometimes

I think Terry is my counselor. Sometimes I think other people are my counselor, too. I don't know how you're supposed to know who your counselor is.

[]

I grew up in a suburb exactly like this one. I know because every suburb is exactly like this one, because every suburb is exactly alike. Our new neighborhood seems quiet and safe, but every first Wednesday of the month all the emergency sirens go off, I guess to remind us all that something terrible could happen at any moment. A coordinated mass shooting by pissed off local teenagers with easy access to AR-15s. An EF-5 tornado like the one in *Twister*. A call from your doctor's office with your lab results. They want to know if now is a good time. They want to know if you have a few minutes.

A few weeks after we moved into this neighborhood, J tried planting grass in the backyard. The seeds were bright blue. She held some in her hand.

"These," she explained to me, "are pre-fertilized seeds."

"And *these*," I explained to her, about what I was holding, "are 3D Crunch Chili Cheese Nacho Doritos."

When the seeds didn't work I tried to act surprised.

"Weird," I said.

The truth is that I have my doubts about some of the basic functionality of our natural world. Photosynthesis.

Cellular Mitosis. The RGB color wheel. It all strikes me as *just a little bit convenient*. I don't think it's fake or anything. I just don't think we're getting the whole story. I've heard if you slice open a cocoon, all you'll find inside is a bunch of Elmer's glue.

Still though. We have to get on with things no matter how far-fetched they may seem. All of life requires a willing suspension of disbelief. Recently I started wearing a neon yellow belt. These are my yellow belt days. My rock and roll days. A small wardrobe adjustment can change your life. I really believe that. I believe all kinds of stupid things. In the morning I strut around the neighborhood waving at everybody like I'm some sort of celebrity. I am, I tell myself, *doing public relations*.

"Hi!" I say.

"Hii!" I say.

I wave with one hand. Then I wave with the other hand.

"Hiiii!!!!" I say.

Most of our neighbors are in their 60s. They water their lawns with hoses. They use some sort of attachment. I don't know where you get attachments. Home Depot, maybe.

"What is that?" I yell at my neighbor, Ken. "Some sort of attachment?"

I strut down Majestic. I strut down Lancelot. I strut down Princess, toward Bob Woodruff Park. I'm getting my struts in. 10,000 struts a day. Doctor recommended.

[]

Cheever says in middle age there is mystery, there is mystification. Lately we've been finding cat shit in the planters. I wonder if this is the mystery he was talking about. Most things are pretty obvious if you stop and think about them. I once asked an atheist why he didn't believe in God. He just shrugged and gestured around at everything.

"Oh," I said. "Right."

Personally, I'm not much for the major world religions these days — the BIG FIVE and all that — but I am a firm believer that any stable, well-functioning adult must be completely out of their goddam mind.

Pascal: "Not to go mad would amount to another form of madness."

Becker: "All character traits are psychosis."

"Faith is being sure of what we hope for and certain of what we do not see," the Bible tells us.

The DSM-5 has another name for this.

[]

In March things cool off. The sky turns greyish. Then it turns grey. J waits a few days. Then she puts pre-fertilized grass seeds into a Scotts Turf Builder® seed spreader and makes laps around the backyard. The blue seeds go flying everywhere, all willy nilly. I watch from the patio with my hands on my hips. "The goal," J explains as she passes back and forth, "is *coverage*." It's a scientific fact that given an excess of chances and opportunities, combined with a lack of planning and know-how, *something* will happen. Lord knows what.

Because our house number is odd, we can only run our sprinklers on Tuesdays and Fridays, but we can use the hose as much as we want. In the evenings, I stand in the backyard watering the blue seeds with an attachment I bought off Amazon. $12. Free shipping. Next-day delivery. I make small movements back and forth to simulate wind and rain.

The goal, I remind myself, is *coverage*.

After a week, the grass starts growing, none of it where it's supposed to, most of it in the planters. I guess we should have seen that one coming.

"Well," J says. "It's not nothing."

"No," I say. "Not nothing."

"It's also not really something, either," she says.

"No," I say. "Definitely not something."

"It's kind of in between, I guess," she says.

"Betweensies," I say.

[]

At thirty-four there's a certain take-what-I-can-get quality to things. Not a lowering of standards, exactly. A *broadening of acceptable outcomes.* I just put my yellow belt on and walk around in circles like everybody else. There's an old saying. *Whatever happens happens.* It's not profound. But I've found that most true things in life are self-explanatory. When I asked the Christian why he thought there was a god, he just shrugged and gestured around at everything.

"Oh," I said. "Right."

[]

On Thursday men with hard hats and facial hair come over to trim the trees in the backyard. Cut some holes for sunlight to get through. Encourage a little goddamn PHOTOSYNTHESIS around here, if you believe in that kind of thing.

"Feel free to get carried away with it, boys!" I yell as they pull the ripcords of their chainsaws. "Trees are stupid!"

"What?!" they yell.

"Nothing!" I yell.

When they're done a few hours later, I can see the sky again, its fake blue color between the sawed-off branches. Just some funny business in atmosphere, I've heard. Refraction or reflection. Something about prisms. I can't remember exactly. A pretty cool trick, though, whatever it is.

In the eighth circle of hell, the false prophets walk backwards, unable to see what's ahead of them. Friday night, I swipe the side mirror off my Nissan Sentra and can no longer see what's behind me. No major loss. I've never been particularly interested in what's going on back there anyway. There's some evidence to suggest that there's no such thing as the past or the future, only the present. The evidence that suggests it is this: *it just kind of feels that way sometimes, doesn't it?*

Friday night, I meet my friend Adam at the 1418 coffee shop in Downtown Plano, a local hipster hotspot where all the customers have Macbook Pros and none of the baristas have heard of decaf. They play alternative Christian music over the speakers and sell a self-published book at the counter called, *Why On Earth Am I Here?* I get the feeling that everyone here is a born again Christian. They're all healthy and clear-eyed and asking about each other's weekends. They're shopping at Old Navy later. They're waking up early tomorrow and going for a jog. I don't know how we're supposed to compete with people who are so thoroughly and enthusiastically out of their minds.

Normally I wouldn't support such an establishment, but they have a lot of parking spaces and their cappuccinos come with pictures of rosetta leaves on top. One day I asked the owner why she called her coffee shop 1418. I figured it was an important historical date. A major turning point in the course of world events. Something, perhaps, had happened in Spain.

"Oh that," she said. "That's just our address."

For all intents and purposes history doesn't exist. Being a person who lacks intentions, who lacks purpose, I might not have even noticed had it not been for the fact that *none of this seems to be going anywhere*. It only makes sense that it didn't come from anywhere either. When I see Adam Friday night it's been four years since we've talked.

"Sorry I'm late," I say. "I swiped the fucking side mirror off my fucking Sentra."

Every few years, I like to check in with my friends and make sure nothing interesting is going on with them. Call it a hobby.

"Same old?" I say.

"Same old," they say.

Lately, though, people have been fucking it up.

"Well…" they say and stare down into their drinks.

Divorce. Unemployment. Sickness. Kids who have begun expressing *a real interest in the arts*. There is no end to the number of ways a perfectly good life can go off the rails. After Adam tells me about his recent health diagnosis — non-fatal but certainly life-altering, the type of diagnosis that makes you question not only your future but also your past — I can't help wondering if this is the part of my life when things start getting pretty weird. When he's done talking, I do what I always do after people tell me things I didn't want to hear. I put my face into my hands and make a low groaning sound into my palms.

"Anything else?" I say, into my palms. "Now's your opportunity."

[]

I live on a cul-de-sac, a dead end, literally the *end of the road*. "No Exit," a sign warns drivers before they turn onto my street. Three or four times a day I watch cars drive past my window. Then, a minute later, they drive past my window again in reverse.

In an attempt to become a healthier, longer-lasting human being, I recently started going on these long walks around my neighborhood, up and down all the fantasy-themed streets, and eventually into Bob Woodruff Park. A mile and a half there, a mile and a half back. Seven thousand steps total. Great for the blood pressure and glucose levels. Last time I had bloodwork done, I had the LDL cholesterol of a man twice my size, the potassium levels of a fourteen-year-old girl, the liver functionality of an aging country music singer.

"Maybe there was a mix up at the lab," I offered the doctor. "Sometimes when the technicians get frisky with each other after hours, they accidentally spill the vials and the blood gets all mixed together. It can lead to some pretty confusing results later on."

My doctor looked at me. Then she asked how many drinks I have per day.

It was hard to say. Not because I didn't know the answer. I just didn't want to say it was all. Like most functioning alcoholics, a large part of my functionality relied on delusion. I knew that. But I also kind of didn't know that, if you know what I mean.

"Let me try asking this more directly," my doctor said. "Are you abusing alcohol?"

"Abusing alcohol?!" I cried. "Absolutely not! Alcohol is abusing me! I'm the victim here!"

After that I started walking regularly, cutting down on sodium, taking daily doses of zinc. I didn't know what zinc did. We had a big bottle of it up in our cupboard. Gummi version. They tasted like Sour Patch Kids. "Zinc time," I said and popped a few. I was hoping that if I could get everything else in my life under control that I could let my drinking stay a little out of control. That I could do a half and half thing.

"Everything in moderation," Geoff Dyer reminds us in *Yoga for People Who Can't Be Bothered to Do It.* "Even moderation itself."

"Wait, you're not doing a half and half thing, are you?" my doctor said a few months later when my numbers hadn't changed. Had gotten worse, actually.

"No," I said.

After that I quit drinking. Then I unquit drinking because I wanted to do a little test. The test involved me drinking again. Then I quit drinking again, the test results having confirmed certain suspicions I had about my drinking, mainly that I was doing it again. Then I unquit drinking again, having forgotten that I'd quit drinking, the whole thing just sort of slipping my mind, probably from all the drinking. Then I bought a book about how to quit drinking. Then I quit drinking.

While walking through Bob Woodruff Park Friday night — four weeks sober, my blood pressure that of a reasonably healthy fifty-year-old man, my zinc-levels that of a South American mineral mine — I pass a large group of geriatric power-walkers dressed in reflective track suits and Nike visors. All of them pumping their elbows side to side. Swinging their hips. Walking backwards. Later I do a little research and learn that walking backwards is the hottest new trend among geriatric suburbanites. The biggest fad since walking forwards. An exciting new way to get where you're going.

I learn something new every day, and it's always something stupid. By thirty-four you've learned all the good lessons already. There's nothing left to learn but stuff you didn't want to know.

"Even if you are well acquainted with walking *forwards*," the article warns, "you will still want to approach walking backwards with caution."

The writer recommends a starting speed of 1 mph.

"If you feel a little out of control," she says. "Try bringing the speed down."

[]

Okay then. Let's try bringing the speed down: Wednesday night J and I go to Ikea to shop for poorly made furniture at unbelievably low prices. They're having a sale. Everything super cheap all the time. This new house we're renting is twice as big as our last place. Two extra rooms. A thousand extra square feet. After we'd moved all our stuff in, we looked around.

"Hmmm," we said.

I don't like the idea of accumulating stuff for no reason, but I also don't like living in a big, empty house. It's echoey in here. There's nothing to sit on. As a compromise, we decide to buy a bunch of cheap Swedish crap that's guaranteed not to last very long. An elegant solution to our problem.

When you buy your furniture at Ikea, you're saying, about your future: "Who knows?" You're saying: "Let's wait and see." You're saying: "The certainty of this coffee table being a meaningful part of my life five years from now is not something I'm willing to bet more than $27 on."

We follow the arrows through the various sections of the store. Bedroom. Bathroom. Office. Miscellaneous items. We imagine that this is our bedroom. We imagine that these are our miscellaneous items. We walk around and around and around and around. I read a news story a few years ago about some kid who re-arranged the arrows inside an Ikea and kept dozens of innocent shoppers trapped for hours.

"We thought we'd never get out," one victim said. "We thought we might live here now."

J and I spend the night assembling particle board shelves and oversized desks using nothing but Allen wrenches and a complete lack of know-how.

"Doesn't exactly seem *made to last*," Graham says when he comes over Saturday and the thing is already falling apart.

"No it does not," I say proudly, smacking the surface with my palm.

That night there's a tornado in the neighborhood. Or the threat of a tornado. A rotation. All the emergency sirens whine like an old-fashioned air raid. The wind between the houses sounds like a Boeing 747 jet engine.

"Don't worry!" I yell at J. "A real tornado sounds like a Union Pacific freight train!"

Your odds of dying at any given moment are .00001%. Your odds of dying at some other moment are 100%.

Not long ago, I came across a man in Bob Woodruff Park who was looking through a telescope. One of those cheap plastic ones you can get from Target for $25. I was a few weeks sober at that point and feeling chatty. It was a nice night. The wind coming from one direction was cold. The wind coming from the other direction was warm. I asked the guy how everything was looking up there in the heavenly realms. How were things hanging in the cosmos these days?

He put his hands on his hips, squinted up at the sky, and shook his head.

"You want the good news?" he said. "Or the bad news?"

Every authentic rebirth is a real ejection from paradise, Earnest Becker reminds us in *The Denial of Death*. A reverse evangelist: Earnest Becker came to tell us the bad news. The bad news is that we're all going to die. The other bad news is that we're all nuts. There is no good news. He was awarded the Pulitzer Prize posthumously in 1974, having died of colon cancer a few months before.

The day Will Smith *smacks the shit* out of Chris Rock at the Academy Awards, I head to Purgatory, to a ski-in ski-out resort at the base of the mountain. It's not a metaphor any more than everything in my life is a metaphor. "As if real life weren't always fiction in the first place," Grégoire Bouillier writes in *The Mystery Guest.* I spend five days in a hot tub floating around in little circles. A zero-gravity simulation at ten thousand feet above sea level. After twenty-four hours I start to feel lightheaded. Mild oxygen deprivation. A freebie high from all the second hand weed in the air. I don't mind.

I used to pay bookoo bucks to feel lightheaded. A head is *heavy*. A head is *awkward*. A head weighs between eight and eleven pounds. They cause all kinds of back problems and posture issues. Most chiropractors recommend against them.

"Something's different about you," J says when I return from Purgatory all stretched out and care-free and no longer having a head.

Today is April 15th in the year of our Lord twenty twenty-two. I'm just kidding. These aren't our lord's years anymore. Surely, they're someone else's at this point. Yesterday Elon Musk offered to buy Twitter for forty-three billion dollars. Maybe these are Elon Musk's years. They're okay. A little uneven. Everything's a little more expensive than it should be. TV's hit or miss. A few days ago, I saw a message on my Nextdoor app. Someone's been going around our neighborhood stealing catalytic converters out of people's cars.

"Keep an eye on your catalytic converters!" the poster warns.

Later I too post a message. Mine's to www.nissanforums.com. "What might one say a catalytic converter is?" my message reads. "And how might one know if one doesn't have one anymore?"

[]

Recently they opened a Jamba Juice near my house. It's

on Spring Creek Blvd and Avenue K, in front of the LA Fitness. Maybe it's been there for a long time. Maybe it's been there for twenty-five years. I don't know. I'm not what you would call *observant*. The other day I drove by it.

"Oh hey," I thought. "Jamba."

Lately it's overcast and humid. Highs in the eighties. Lows in the eighties. Some real Jamba Juice weather if you know what I mean. I'm going to Jamba Juice a lot. That's what I mean. Once or twice a week. There's a constant chance of rain but never any rain. A bold-faced refutation of statistics and probability. As if all of us didn't already have our doubts. In the morning I put on my yellow belt and look at myself in the bathroom mirror.

"Showtime," I say.

I'm ten weeks sober, slightly dehydrated, completely headless with a mild iron deficiency and a low-to-nonexistent sperm count. I may or may not be operating without the assistance of a catalytic converter. In my experience we all need a little less than we think. Carl says when he lived in Los Angeles he dated a girl who was missing her large intestine.

"Cool," I said.

"Her mouth was connected directly to her asshole," he said.

"Wonderful," I said.

"Five minutes after Waffle House it was *Welcome to Shit Town, USA*," he said.

Once he had to pull over on the side of the highway,

etc. A colostomy bag, etc. Wet wipes in the glove box, etc. He would have married her too, he told me, if she hadn't been so religious.

"Trini*tar*ians," he said.

The day before Easter, one thousand nine hundred and eighty-nine years after the crucifixion of Christ, twenty-four hours before the anniversary of his resurrection, we drive to J's parents' house in West Plano, across US75, near the H Mart. On the way over we stop at Texaco for gas. $3.95 a gallon.

"Gas prices have risen," I say.

"They have risen indeed," J says.

Recently an op-ed in *Bloomberg* encouraged Americans who make less than $300,000 a year to stop eating meat.

"Try lentils," the writer suggested.

We all have to make sacrifices. In the story of Christianity, Jesus sacrifices himself to save us all from Hell. In the story of *Avengers: Endgame*, Iron Man sacrifices himself to save us all from space lizards. Me, though, I prefer the type of stories where we're all fucked no matter what.

"Have you heard the Good News?" a Christian once asked me on a train in Downtown Dallas.

"Yes," I said. "Have you heard the bad news?"

Saturday afternoon we sit around my in-laws' kitchen table in West Plano eating gluten-free French toast and low sodium bacon. We drink Sprite and grape juice mixed together. To commemorate the resurrection of our Lord and Savior Jesus Christ, we are each given a hollow chocolate bunny.

"The secret," my six-year-old niece whispers to me, "is to start with the head."

[]

The forecast this week is all hot air and inflation. Ups and downs. Monday morning, I go for my daily walk through my neighborhood. Everyone around me is all hunched over and trudging along under the weight of their big, stupid heads. Straining their necks and shoulders. Trying to keep those things level with the horizon.

It's eighty degrees out. Overcast. Humid like a car wash. In a clearing by the pond, I come across a hot air balloon. It's being inflated. I wonder if this is the inflation the forecast was talking about.

"Bigger!" I yell as it grows above the trees, an eighty-foot-tall technicolor bounce house.

"What?!" they yell.

"Nothing!" I yell as the hot air balloon lifts off the ground carrying three old men in windbreakers up above the power lines.

[]

This neighborhood we're in is mostly retirees, community college students, amateur power walkers, and other people in various stages of completely giving up on their lives. Around 6pm the whole neighborhood smells like Stouffer's lasagna and Ore-Ida crinkle cut fries. Around 9pm it smells like chamomile and weed. Five square blocks of people taking it easy. Every community can be a retirement community if its residents lack enough ambition. Up in Purgatory there was a sign on our cabin wall. "It's all downhill from here, folks," it said.

To keep my blood sugar down, I take 14mgs of insulin glargine a day, injected directly into the fatty part of my stomach. To keep my blood pressure down I take a small pink pill. I don't know what it does. It's so small and pink it's hard to believe it does anything. Just to be safe, I take two. Common side effects include fatigue, irritability, dry mouth, disorientation, extreme light headedness. In some cases, your head just floats off completely. It's been known to happen.

"Hmmmm," my doctor says when I go in for my annual checkup and I don't have a head. "That's weird."

Much like the appendix, coccyx, catalytic converter, 94th Academy Awards, and the entire field of weather prediction and meteorology, experts are still not *one hundred percent certain* what the human head is for. One theory is that it's some sort of battery.

[]

I don't know how much a gallon of milk costs in the year of Elon Musk 2022 but a large Razzmatazz™ from Jamba Juice costs $6.59 plus tax.

I add a boost of vitamin C for my immune system. A boost of vitamin D for an overall sunny disposition. I avoid the boost of vitamin E, a known memory enhancer. None of this strikes me as being particularly worth remembering. Not worth the extra $1 if you catch my drift.

I sit outside Jamba Juice on their rattly metal chairs, the ones designed to withstand nuclear Armageddon, 120-degree temperatures, teenagers who drive used Camaros and connect their wallets to their pants with chains. I wobble back and forth, working my hip flexors and lower back. I wonder if I've invented a new hip exercise. Biceps be damned. I'm all *hips*, baby.

"Have you seen that guy's hips?" I imagine people saying. "*Powerful.*"

The Razzmatazz™ tastes like sherbet and bananas. It feels like vitamin C and vitamin D. I can feel my immune system boosting. I can feel my disposition getting sunnier. It's late afternoon. Eighty degrees with a chance of rain. I suck a banana chunk through the straw as a hot air balloon goes floating by overhead, low and getting lower, all cool air and deflation, the pattern on the outside bright red and pixelated like when I was a kid and I used to press my face right up against the TV screen, so close my eyelashes would pop with static electricity.

"LOWER!" I yell as the balloon descends into Bob Woodruff Park. "BRING HER DOWN NICE AND EASY, BOYS!"

In the basket I can see the three old men in windbreakers, wide-eyed and sunburned, white beards down to their chests, heads bobbling around, looking like three Moseses come down the mountain and we all need to have a little chat.

I once heard someone say that every life contains the entire human experience. It turns out the experience just isn't that complicated is all. Joy. Sadness. Highs and lows. By three-years-old, you've pretty much gotten the idea.

Monday night Molly comes over and we pull tarot cards from her garden-themed deck. Every card related back to Mother Earth. Shrubs. Bushes. Trees. Grass. Some real woo woo shit but I don't mind. I'll go along with pretty much anything. It's one of my deepest philosophical convictions that everything is pretty much whatever.

"You're a magical tree in a cupcake forest!" my niece told me the other day.

"Okay!" I said.

Molly fans the cards like a magician, and I pull the six of wands. It has six wands on it. A man standing in what looks to be some sort of backyard in a medieval suburb. We stare at the card for a while. Then we look it up online. The six of wands, we learn, is all about trusting your instincts, listening to your heart, deciding what's right for you.

Is what you're doing really worth doing? The card seems to be asking.

It's a good question. I've been wondering that myself lately. I've also been wondering the opposite of that. Is what I'm not doing worth not doing? I'm four months sober. Not a drop of booze since February. An honest-to-God miracle. Recently a family member asked me what I've been doing with myself lately.

"More like what haven't I been doing!" I said.

"Okay," they said. "What haven't you been doing?"

"That's private," I said.

[]

Last month someone started painting arrows on all the sidewalks in the neighborhood. At lunch, the dog and I follow them around. They take us down Royal Oaks to Princess Blvd. Then over to Camelot. Then over to Guinevere. They're poorly done. Freehand. White spray paint on concrete. Some of them look like lower case R's. Some of them look like capital T's. I think if you're looking for signs in your life, you can't be too picky about what they are. I think — if you're looking for signs in your life — you kind of have to take what you can get.

"Well," I say when we find another arrow pointing us deeper into the neighborhood. "Good enough for me."

It's May now. The tree pollen is moderate. The ragweed pollen is moderate. The grass pollen is high. Everybody I know is whacked out on Flonase and Claritin D. Even the dog takes a small dose. An entire city experiencing the common side effects of over-the-counter antihistamines. Drowsiness. Fatigue. Irritability. Constant, low-level confusion about what's going on. Yesterday some guy knocked on my front door.

"I need money for the cleaning lady," he said.

It seemed like an odd request considering I didn't know this guy and had no idea what he was talking about. Still though. The cleaning lady needed to be paid. A lot of people are paycheck to paycheck these days. Most Americans are not prepared to handle a financial emergency of more than a thousand dollars. I heard about it on a podcast.

"How much does she need?" I said.

"How should I know?" he said.

Around then I realized I was talking to my mentally disabled neighbor, Ken. He lives across the street with his mentally disabled brother, Eddie. They take care of each other. It's kind of sweet if you're into that sort of thing.

"Hang on," I said. "Let me put my shoes on."

I shuffled over there and talked to the cleaning lady who was young and friendly and just as confused as me.

"They can just pay me next time," she said. "It's no problem."

"You can just pay her next time," I told Ken. "I've worked it all out for you. It's not a problem."

[]

This is our second summer in this house on Majestic Circle. We like it here okay. It's middle class, middle brow, smack in the middle of Middle America. Everyone here drives a pre-owned Honda Accord and weedwacks constantly, two or three times a week. At any given time, on any given day, somebody in our neighborhood is engaged in some form of landscaping. I read in *Scientific American* that America's most-grown crop is the front lawn.

The main reason we moved into this fantasy-themed neighborhood was because J got a job teaching history at the high school down the street. Educating today's youth on the various goings on of our forefathers and foremothers. She wears themed T-shirts depending on what they're learning that day. On Tuesday it's a Richard Nixon T-shirt. On Wednesday it's Roe V. Wade. On Friday it's a picture of an American soldier in Vietnam.

"War is hell," his helmet says.

Maybe they all say that.

I don't know very much about America. I'm not sure anybody does. The shirts aren't helping. Yesterday she was wearing a shirt with a pineapple on it. This morning it was an atomic bomb.

Sometimes when J gets frustrated about the way things are going around here, with our loosey goosey gun laws, looming environmental catastrophes, and backyards that refuse to grow even a single blade of grass, she talks about moving back up to Toronto.

"Can I come?" I say.

"No," she says. "You'll just slow me down."

[]

These are the first days of summer. Overcast and damp. Highs in the 90s. Lows in the 80s. A chance of rain with a certainty of being miserable. There's some comfort in the reliability of it. Most lab rats prefer constant abuse to unpredictability.

Yesterday I found a dead bluebird in the backyard. A victim of heat stroke and dehydration. The latest casualty of our slowly warming planet. I put out an old Tupperware container filled with tap water and declared myself our neighborhood's Minister of Wildlife Hydration.

"Just as the Lord cares for the birds of the air, so will he care for you," the Bible tells us.

I know, I think. *That's what I'm afraid of.*

In the evenings I sit on the back patio reading news.google.com on my phone and drinking Topo Chico out of a beer glass. At some point the neighbor kid starts jumping on the trampoline. He lives over there with his grandparents. Or maybe he just visits sometimes. I hear the sound of springs and then see his head start popping up over the fence.

"Hey," he says.

"Hey," I say.

"Do you have a dog?" he says.

"Yeah," I say.

"Is it a real dog or a robot dog?" he says.

"It's a real dog," I say.

"Oh," he says. "I thought maybe it was a robot dog."

Kids these days seem dumb but, like you, I'm putting a tremendous amount of faith in them. I sit out here until the mosquitos show up. Asian Tigers. The ones with the white stripes on their backs. Marsha told me about them. She says they feed all day and all night. Blood thirsty alcoholics. However much they get, they always want a little more. Like me, they showed up on the scene completely uncalled for some time in the 80s. And, like me, they're capable of drinking themselves to death.

"I don't remember these from when I was a kid," J says, smacking one against her ankle.

"Yeah," I say. "These are new."

Recently on my Nextdoor app, I heard about a plan to release ten million sterile mosquitos into the neighborhood to help control the population. Decoy fuck toys to keep these things occupied. Mass extinction after a single generation. A ridiculous plan but I've heard worse. I watched a TED talk a few years ago about a device that would shoot mosquitos out of the air with laser beams. Powered by AAA batteries. You could hang it on your porch like a windchime.

[]

On Tuesday J wears the Nixon shirt again. On Wednesday it's Roe V. Wade. History repeating itself. A three-week laundry cycle. It's not like I thought we were getting anywhere but a little variety would be nice.

"Give us a little *razzle dazzle*," I suggest. "*Surprise us.*"

Now that I'm halfway through my thirties, very likely halfway through my life — here at the midpoint of this amateur musical theater production of my existence — I'm faced with the very real possibility that I've already gotten the gist. That I more or less get what's going on here. That there's nothing left to do but make art and walk around in circles and try to act surprised when everything I know is going to happen eventually happens.

Try, I mean, to appreciate all of this *for what it is.*

[]

At a dinner party Sunday night, Molly makes gluten-free lasagna and low-sodium Caesar salad. Everyone with their *sensitivities*. Everyone with their *restrictions*. Cutting something out. Adding something in. She puts red grapes in one bowl and green grapes in a different bowl. Chili in one pot, vegetarian chili in another. As an appetizer, she serves CVS-brand acid reducers.

"Now that we're all middle-aged," she says.

Not that I need reminding. Recently my sister texted me the results of her latest colonoscopy. It seems the doctors didn't like what they found up there.

"Well what did they think they were going to find up there?" I said. "Something *likeable*?"

It's possible our expectations for what we'll find up our butts might be a tad high.

"What I'm trying to tell you," my sister said, "is that it might be a good idea to schedule yours sooner rather than later."

"And what I'm trying to tell you," I said, "is that there is a big difference between what people tell me and what I choose to hear."

[]

Weeks later, the geniuses over at NASA post a picture to Twitter of the deepest, darkest part of the known universe captured in ultra-high definition by the ten-billion-dollar James Webb Space Telescope.

"There it is," they say.

"There it is," we say.

That afternoon my doctor emails me JPEGs of the deepest, darkest parts of my large intestine, all the way up my own ass, a place I've been slowly crawling for the better part of four decades.

"There it is," he says.

"There it is," I say.

Later I follow the arrows around the neighborhood again. I don't think they're going anywhere but it's something to do. Most of life is just us killing time, you know? Or maybe it's the other way around.

I follow the arrows down Queens Way to Merlin Drive. Then down Camelot to Guinevere. Then into the Bowman Russel cemetery, smack in the middle of the subdivision. Final resting place of thirty or forty people who never made it out of the neighborhood. A common enough fate. I looked it up: There are twenty-two cemeteries in Plano, fifty-thousand cemeteries in Texas, one-hundred-and-fifty-thousand cemeteries in the United States. Wherever you're standing, you're probably standing in a cemetery. I've heard that no matter where you dig, you'll eventually hit bone.

2601

Chris and Inga were getting a new couch and they'd offered to give us their old one. A genuine leather three-cushion from some fancy store like Restoration Hardware or Ethan Allen. All we had to do was pick it up. Easier said than done. I would know. I'm something of an expert when it comes to saying things and not doing them. I say things all the time. Have yet to do anything. The saying, I tell myself, is enough.

In this case, though, I considered making an exception. For years I'd admired Chris and Inga's couch and had sometimes fantasized about owning one just like it someday. An oversized, overstuffed lump of a thing, roughly the same size as the cow it had been made from. A piece of high-end, luxury furniture that I felt communicated not only comfort and leisure but also financial excess.

It made sense that Chris and Inga would have a couch like this since they are, by far, our most comfortable, leisurely, and financially excessive friends. He works for a computer company. She works for a bank. They live in a town called — I'm not kidding — *Prosper.*

Even here in our mid-to-late thirties, we're still living on the hand-me-down generosity of our older, more successful friends. The trickledown economics of late-capitalist social circles.

"Yours if you want it," Chris had texted me along with a picture of the couch sitting in his garage.

[]

The Saturday before my thirty-fifth birthday, on a hot morning in June, we rented a twenty-foot U-Haul truck with a cartoon alien head painted on the side. A tribute to the dried-up beauty of the New Mexican desert. Part of U-Haul's decade-long ad campaign designed to celebrate all the different places it's possible to live, as if any place is just as good as any other.

Prosper is thirty minutes away from us. Not close. Not far. A straight shot up the President George Bush Turnpike. Then over to the Dallas North Tollway. You pay $4.56 in tolls. You drive past three golf courses, thirty-seven churches, five indoor malls, two of which are abandoned and being replaced with trendy new apartment complexes. You drive past two Super Targets, two Neighborhood Walmart's, three Chili's. You drive past Ikea.

While we drove, we couldn't help noticing all the other U-Hauls on the road around us. All of us driving our big, empty trucks out to Prosper to pick up our rich friends' hand-me-downs. When we're done with them, years from now, we'll put them out on our curbs for people a little bit poorer than us to pick up and take further south, down to Dallas. Then down to Houston. Then down to El Paso. I don't know where it'll all go after that. South America would make sense.

"I'm just now realizing something," J said, her hands in a death grip at ten and two. "Every time you see a U-Haul on the road, it's being driven by somebody who has very little experience driving a U-Haul and is probably stressed out of their fucking mind."

"There should really be some type of screening process involved," I said.

"A background check," she said. "A questionnaire."

"One question: *Are you sure about this?*"

"A *yes* checkbox, and a *no* checkbox."

Chris and Inga live in the type of upper-middle-class neighborhood you can only find if you know where to look for it. It's like that island in *Pirates of the Caribbean*. You make a left turn and then a right turn and then a right turn again. You loop around a traffic circle a few times. You type a code into a thing. Suddenly you're in a luxury subdivision with a tractor theme. It smells like hairspray and grilled cheese sandwiches. All the lawns are electric green with cross-hatched mower lines. All the children drive golf carts. Around here, the curbs are rounded off and the speed bumps are gently sloped. A neighborhood with no hard edges, no discomforts, no surprises.

Once, while Chris and Inga were building their house out here, they'd invited us to walk around the place before the dry wall went up. There was nothing but a foundation and a frame, so you could move between the walls like a ghost. The kitchen, the bedrooms, the living room, the garage. I stood there pretending like it all made sense to me, like I could picture what this place would be like when it was done, but the whole time I mostly just felt weirded out. I've always felt weirded out by houses that aren't quite finished being built. When you can see for yourself that all these houses we put so much faith in are made out of nothing but wood and nails and a bunch of cheap crap you can buy at Home Depot. I don't know what I was hoping they'd be made out of. Something more official, I guess.

After J parked the U-Haul in front of Chris and Inga's house, I texted Chris to see if he could back this thing in for us. A lot of people are too proud to ask for help. Not me. I'll ask anyone to help me do anything. There is no problem so small I won't ask someone else to handle it for me.

"Here," I say. "You look like you'd be good at this."

So Chris backed the U-Haul into the driveway for us, and then his kids helped us lift the couch into the back. I'll admit I have sometimes wondered what kids are for, so it was nice to see a practical application for them.

"Oh," I thought. "They're for lifting."

We were halfway home when I realized we'd created a new problem for ourselves. We'd had Chris's kids load the coach in. Now we were going to have to unload it ourselves. For every problem you solve, a new problem is created. Sometimes I wonder if it would be easier to just learn to live with the problems you already have. Save yourself a step.

We pulled the U-Haul into our neighborhood and parked in front of our house. Then we sat there for a while. I wondered if this was one of those problems that would eventually take care of itself. It seemed worth finding out. We must have been sitting there awhile because eventually our neighbor Ken knocked on the window.

"Moving out?" he said.

"No," we said. "New couch."

We opened up the back and showed him.

"Looks kinda beat up," he said.

"Yeah," I said. "Technically it's garbage."

He stood there for a minute. Then he walked back home and got his brother, Eddie. I'd never met Eddie before, but I'd seen him around the neighborhood. Like me, he spends a lot of time wandering around in circles with his headphones on and his hands in his pockets. He looked strong, though, like the type of guy who was about to come in handy. I'll admit I have sometimes wondered what other people are for, so it was nice to see a practical application for them.

"Lifting," I thought again.

Even with four full-grown adults working at it, the couch was still hard to move. It was almost like it didn't want to move. An object at rest and all that. Nothing wants to go anywhere. Everything wants to stay put. It's one of the laws of the universe. The second one, I think.

Eventually, though, we managed to shove the couch off the truck and onto the curb. Then we managed to cartwheel it onto the front lawn. Then we slid it across the front lawn to the front door. Then we shoved it through the front door. Nothing wants to go anywhere, but you can always try giving things a shove. Sometimes shoving them works. After five or six moves, our new couch was sitting in our living room, and we were sitting on it. The couch, I'm happy to report, seemed to be working.

We all sat there for a minute, out of breath, staring at the wall.

"So," Ken said finally, drumming his fingers on his knees. "What are you gonna do with your old one?"

There was an ambulance parked outside my neighbor's house the other day. This morning it was a purple sedan with the name of a funeral home on the side of it.

"147 Fatalities on Dallas Roads This Year," a light-up sign on US75 reminds unsuspecting drivers. "Buckle Up, Y'all."

When people say there are no atheists in foxholes, I wonder if they've looked around. It all looks like a foxhole to me.

Not long after we moved into this house, we noticed a crack running through the middle of it. It started near the front door and ran all the way back into the kitchen. J marked the end of it with a pencil. When it grew past the mark, we called our property management company, a small business that shares its name with a crime fighting dog. They sent out a guy with a tape measure and a little black box. He set the box in the middle of the room and stepped back.

"Lasers," he said.

"Cool," I said.

Since we don't own this house, we never found out the results of those tests. We never even found out what the tests were for. ("I don't have any answers!" a student once wailed to J. "I don't even have any questions!"). Nothing too serious, I hope. I'd like to think if this house was falling apart, we'd get an email about it. As it is, we just keep going about our lives with this thin, black line creeping its way through the middle of everything like that Edgar Allen Poe story. It's not out of the ordinary. In Texas, every house has foundation problems. It literally *comes with the territory*. I was familiar with the benefits and drawbacks of pier-and-beam by age nine. Around here responsible homeowners run soaker hoses around their foundations six-to-seven hours a day. Not cheap but cheaper than the alternative. I learned about it from our next door neighbor, a guy who owns a landscaping company.

"Every idiot knows that," he said, about the soaker hoses.

"Not every idiot," I said.

[]

It's fall now. Rainy and cool. There's a mud puddle in our backyard the size of a mattress. After a year of throwing grass seeds around back here, we finally gave up. Now we have this mud puddle. I don't mind. Mud is natural. Mud is clean. I've heard that every mud puddle, no matter how small, contains the same ingredients as the one we crawled out of four billion years ago. Amino acid and hydroxic acid.

Polypeptides, they're called.

I read about them in a science magazine.

[]

Lately J and I have been thinking about buying a house of our own. Thirteen years of renting places. Maybe it's time to own one. We go to Chili's and discuss our options. City or suburbs. One story or two stories. Brick or wood. Tudor, ranch style, Dutch colonial.

One problem with buying a house is that I don't really want one. Another problem is how expensive they are. I looked it up. They cost three-hundred-thousand dollars. That seems a little pricey for something I don't want.

"Where are we supposed to get three-hundred-thousand dollars?" I ask J.

"That's what a *mortgage* is for," she says.

Even though I work for a mortgage company, I don't know very much about them. I know they're very popular, and I know they're very expensive. They were invented by banks sometime in the 1930s, right around the time that William J. Levitt invented the American suburbs and James Truslow Adams invented The American Dream.

"That dream of a land in which life should be better and richer and fuller for everyone," Truslow wrote in *The Epic of America.*

In my job interview at the mortgage company, a guy in khaki pants asked if I knew what the word mortgage meant.

"Death contract," he said before I could answer.

You're more likely to die than pay one off.

[]

I don't have any answers. I don't even have any questions. The crack through the house keeps getting bigger, but I'm not too worried about it. I'm not too worried about anything. I try to accept my circumstances with the nonchalance of a man who doesn't think any of it is really his problem. The hands-off approach of a lifelong renter.

God grant me the serenity to accept the things I cannot change, I think. *And the wisdom to know that I pretty much can't change anything.*

In the morning, I pop a chalky pink blood pressure pill and brush my teeth with an electric toothbrush that harnesses the power of sound. I inject myself with an artificial insulin I've heard is derived from pigs. I put on my yellow belt, the color of pure American electricity, and walk to Bob Woodruff and back. In the 18 months we've lived here, I've walked 466 laps around our fantasy-themed neighborhood. 3,527,637 steps. 1,406 miles. Dallas to Toronto and then some.

At night I lay on my genuine leather couch drinking chamomile tea. I'm ten months off booze, four years off soda, but I'm not above a little *chemical assistance* now and then. We buy the tea with the bear on the box. He's in his pajamas. He's getting sleepy. After an hour I start getting sleepy too. Effects as advertised. The benefits of extra-strength chamomile and a life-long avoidance of responsibility. I lay my phone down on my chest and stare up at the crack in the ceiling. It's getting bigger still. Wide enough now to insert dimes. Soon it will be wide enough to insert silver dollars. I don't know what to do about a house that's cracking in half. I don't know if they sell something for that. Some sort of glue maybe. Outside I hear sirens. They get closer and closer. Then they get further and further away. A Doppler-effect pitch bend. Rock and roll.

I was laid up with a bad case of Covid recently when I came across an article in an old *National Geographic* magazine that said people have been around for seven million years. All that time and it's still not clear what we're all doing here or what we're all for. At this point, I'm afraid to ask.

For Christmas my father-in-law gave me a copy of a book by Wendell Barry called *What Are People For?* I guess he could tell I'd been wondering. I thanked him for the book, put it on my shelf, but didn't read it. Haven't read it still. So it would be fair to question how badly I really want to know.

Tuesday night I get coffee with my writer friend, Nathan. A few years ago he wrote a book about why believing in God is still, here in the twenty-first century, a perfectly reasonable thing to do. Still perfectly *sane*. Six months ago he was diagnosed with stage 4 colon cancer. Thirty-five fucking years old. Now he says he can only write poetry.

"Poetry and music," he says.

We get coffee at the Starbucks off Mockingbird Lane, by the Urban Outfitters. J and I used to live over here, in a semi-famous apartment complex called The Phoenix. It was well-known in the area for these huge art deco murals on its exterior walls. Four story depictions of young Dallasites in various states of being out on the town. They were riding Vespas. They were listening to jazz. As far as I know, nobody in Dallas has ever ridden a vespa or listened to jazz but back then we all still thought we might.

Our apartment was on the first floor, but because the complex had been built on a hill it was also kind of on the second floor too. An Escherian mindfuck: you could enter our building on the first floor, go up a floor, and still be on the first floor.

I was telling Nathan about it Tuesday night while we sat outside on the Starbucks patio, watching storm clouds roll in over US75. Towering thunderheads the size of five-thousand-story-buildings. Later some trees in my neighborhood would get knocked over. Some houses would lose power. People would have to reprogram their coffee pots. It would be, all in all, kind of annoying.

"Does all of it matter?" I asked Nathan after we'd sat there in silence for a while. "Or does none of it matter?"

It wasn't an elegant question to ask a sick man, but I really needed to know. I hoped that his recent diagnosis had given him access to this kind of knowledge. And I hoped the fact that I didn't know him very well meant

I was allowed to ask.

"Why does everyone keep asking me that?" he said.

[]

It's springtime in the Metroplex. I've been listening to jazz. Nothing fancy. The basics. *Monk's Dream*. *Kind of Blue*. This Coltrane one that he recorded back in 1963 and they only just released. *Both Directions at Once*, it's called, after a conversation Coltrane had with saxophone player Wayne Shorter.

"We talked about doing impossible things on your instrument," Shorter said in an interview. "We talked about starting a sentence in the middle and then going to the beginning and the end at the same time."

In the evening, I put on Coltrane, pour a Topo Chico into a beer glass, and sit outside on the back patio. We get three or four nice days a year here in Plano. Big, blue skies. Temperatures in the 60s and 70s. A day like this comes along every few months and none of us can ever believe it. We call each other up.

"Can you believe this day we're having?" we say.

I'm not sure we can. I'm not sure we *should*. After four to six months of rain, hail, and snow — not to mention twenty to thirty years of heat, droughts, and tornados — a nice day does seem a little far-fetched.

Back when J and I lived in that apartment on Mockingbird Lane — our last place in the city before we moved to the suburbs — we used to sit out on our balcony on nice nights like this, smoking Marlboro

Reds and drinking Bulleit bourbon out of plastic cups. Our complex had been built on the site of an old Dr Pepper factory. In the summertime, when the sidewalks got hot, people said you could still smell the twenty-three flavors of America's third favorite soft drink seeping out of the ground. Almond, vanilla, blackberry, caramel, apricot, plum, etc. Now J and I live in a neighborhood that smells like lawn mowers and hot dogs. An old neighborhood full of old people. The trees are old. The cars are old. And J and I, we're getting old too.

Older, let's say.

On Wednesday I go in for my latest in-office health screening and score a 7.1 out of 10. My official health status in the eyes of my company is: NOT BAD. During the exam, the nurse heard something funny rattling around inside my lungs. Leftovers from Covid, I assumed, and whatever long-term damage those Marlboro Reds did all those years ago. Just to be safe, she sent me to get my chest X-rayed at one of these places people go to get bad news. The Texas Oncology Center off Plano Parkway.

"I'm here for my bad news," I tell the receptionist when I check in the next day.

She stares at me.

"I'm here for my chest X-ray," I say again, a little quieter.

Sometimes I forget that not everybody's life is a huge joke. Sometimes I forget that some people are taking this seriously.

After I sign in, the nurse points me to the waiting area,

which is full of seventy- and eighty-year-olds with walkers and canes and oxygen tanks. I wonder if there's been some sort of mix-up. I'm thirty-five-fucking-years-old. Fourteen months sober. Semi-vegetarian with every intention of going gluten free. I've eaten nothing but lentils and mackerel for an entire year. Not healthy, exactly, but healthy *as can be*. Twenty minutes later in the back room, I pose shirtless in front of a white plastic wall while they project a laser-sight bullseye at the center of my chest.

"You'll get your bad news by Monday," the receptionist says, straight faced, when I check out. "Friday at the latest."

[]

I don't mind waiting around for bad news. In *some ways*, it's all I've ever really been doing. In some ways, it's all I've ever really done. Working and walking around in circles and putting together Ikea furniture but mostly waiting around for bad news. An Escherian mindfuck: I never saw any of this going anywhere anyway.

[]

Saturday night J and I babysit our nieces up in McKinney. Six and nine. Both of them have moonbeams shooting out of their faces. That's how I can tell them apart from other kids. If they ever get lost in a crowd, I'll just look for the moonbeams. On the off chance that both of their parents die together in some freak car accident or plane crash, our nieces will come live with me and J. Legal guardianship they call it. It's all very official.

My nieces live in a new neighborhood with a space theme. All the trees are new. All the families are new. It smells like chlorine and McDonald's French fries. Everyone has bright red popsicle stains around their mouths. When you pull in, you have to swerve around all the kids' bikes that have been left in the street. Then you have to swerve around all the kids. They're covered in sugar and mud. They're covered in polypeptides. J and I aren't passionate about bringing new kids into the world, but we're quite fond of the ones who are already here. We might as well try to make them feel at home. Try, if we can, to take them seriously.

"Do scientists know where God is?" my niece asked my brother-in-law recently.

"Well," he said, "Not all scientists believe in God."

"I'm a scientist," she said. "I believe in God."

[]

On Thursday, I'll get a call from my doctor's office with the results of my tests. They'll ask if now is a good time. They'll ask if I have a few minutes. Until then, I walk around in a quantum realm where I am both perfectly healthy and a total goner. Where I have six months to live or sixty years. The still point between two futures. Moving in both directions at once. Before you open Schrödinger's box, the cat is both dead and alive.

Not really. But also yes really.

In the meantime, I sit out on my patio in the evenings listening to Coltrane, reading Wendell Barry, drinking coffee way past 7pm. The weather isn't nice but it's as nice as can be. I don't mind. I'm happiest when I have something to complain about. Here's something: I've read two hundred pages of this *What Are People For?* book and still don't know the answer. Still don't even know what this book is *about*. Not that that's always a bad thing. Most of my favorite books aren't about anything. I'm suspicious of clarity and focus. In this case, however, a simple answer would have been nice.

[]

At some point the dog wanders out onto the patio, and then the cat wanders out onto the patio, and then J wanders out here, too. She brings her book and her blanket and her Sleepytime tea. Somewhere in the neighborhood somebody's grilling hot dogs. Somewhere somebody's wacking weeds. I sneeze and hear a child's voice from the backyard next door say, "God bless you."

"I'm getting eaten alive out here," J says after two or three minutes, smacking Asian Tigers off her ankles, gathering up all her stuff and going back inside.

"Me too," I say, and then just keep sitting out here on the porch swing until the streetlights come on and the June bugs come out and all the houses in the neighborhood start to glow.

May 2023
Plano, Texas

Acknowledgements

Parts of this book originally appeared—sometimes unrecognizably—in *Little Engines, Peach Mag, Hobart, HAD, Identity Theory, Farewell Transmission,* and *Word West Revue.*

Thank you to the early readers: J. D. Daniels, Amy Fusselman, and Adam Voith. Thank you to Michael Wheaton, who has become not only a trusted editor and publisher but a good friend. Thank you to the amazingly talented Amy Wheaton. Thank you to everyone who let me use their name and likeness. Or sometimes just their name. Or sometimes just their likeness. Thank you to my best friend, J.

Thank you, thank you, thank you.

About the Author

Mike Nagel is the author of *Duplex* (Autofocus Books, 2022). His essays have appeared in *DIAGRAM, Salt Hill, X-R-A-Y,* and *The Paris Review Daily.* He lives in Texas.

[a]

— also from Autofocus Books —

Duplex — Mike Nagel

XO — Sara Rauch

Until It Feels Right — Emily Costa

Cleave — Holly Pelesky

Nextdoor in Colonialtown — Ryan Rivas

Too Much Tongue — Adrienne Marie Barrios & Leigh Chadwick

Picture Window — Danny Caine

the nature machine! — Tyler Gillespie

A Kind of In-Between — Aaron Burch

How to Write a Novel: An Anthology of 20 Craft Essays About Writing, None of Which Ever Mention Writing — ed. Aaron Burch

Hiraeth — Mistie R. Watkins

That Spell — Tate N. Oquendo

My Modest Blindness — Russell Brakefield

A Calendar Is A Snakeskin — Kristine Langley Mahler